RETRACTION

Christopher van Ginhoven Rey

RETRACTION

TEOREMA

Published by Teorema
Los Angeles, CA
http://teorema.press

ISBN: 979-8-9938748-1-4

Library of Congress Control Number: 2025923814

Printed in the United States of America

O death, where is your victory?

I COR. 15:55

THE MAN MADE no mention of the fact that the village was right next to the border. I was the one who, at some point during our conversation, decided to look it up on the map. I don't know why I bothered doing that since by then I'd already told the man I'd be happy to meet him there. I wasn't going to back out after that. I would have had to explain why I'd changed my mind, and that was something I really had no desire to do.

§

Later, while going over the conversation in my head, I found myself wondering if the omission had been an oversight. I'd assumed that to be the case, but the more I thought about it, the less certain I felt. It just struck me as unlikely that someone would forget to mention something so important. At the same time, it wasn't like the man had much to say about the village. It was almost as if, as far as he was concerned, its name were all I needed to know.

§

He might have been right. For the purposes of getting there, the village's name would have probably sufficed. I'd told the man I'd be taking the bus. Technically, all I needed to do was check the timetable at the stop. Still, I would have appreciated being told where I was headed. One shouldn't just assume that someone will be willing to meet near a border, least of all a foreigner.

I WAS ABOUT to get ready for bed when he called. I usually have my phone on silent by then, so I was surprised when I heard it ring. To be perfectly honest, when I saw it was him, I decided not to pick up. I remember staring at his name, flashing up on the screen with each ring. I must not have felt like talking—not for any specific reason, at least not as far as I can remember. I think I just wasn't in the mood.

§

I changed my mind in the end, I'm not sure why. By then the phone had been ringing for a while. The man was probably expecting the call to go to my voicemail—I remember it took him a few seconds to respond to my greeting, as if he first wanted to make sure it was really me on the other end of the line. This hesitation was perfectly understandable. It can be awkward to realize you've been talking to a pre-recorded message—even when no one else is around, there's always something slightly embarrassing about it.

§

Considering how I'd been feeling, the conversation got off to a good start. I asked the man what he'd been up to since I'd last seen him, and he replied that he hadn't been doing very much. He'd gone to a play the night before, along with some friends. He told me about it, but without going into much detail; he just gave me a general idea of the plot. I said it sounded interesting, which was true. Then he asked me how I was doing. I told him I was okay, just a bit tired. That was also true.

§

It wasn't long before he mentioned the village. He wanted to know if it would be possible for us to meet there. I told him I had no problem with that, without giving it too much thought. Being relatively new to the area, I really had no idea where he was asking me to go.

.

BY THE TIME I found out, we had already moved on to another topic. The man was saying something, I can't remember what exactly, but it didn't seem like he would be stopping anytime soon, so I decided to put him on speakerphone, just so I could look at the map.

§

Having learned where the village was, I could have asked him if he would be willing to meet somewhere else. I didn't, though, and not because by then I'd gotten used to meeting men in all kinds of places—unlikely places, some of them: only a few days ago, I'd met someone in a cave, amid the ruins of a Roman temple. This wasn't that kind of meeting, by which I mean the kind of meeting I've come to expect, since arriving in this part of the world, to take place in a strange, even improbable, location. I didn't say anything simply because, as I mentioned earlier, I didn't want to have to explain myself. Based on my experience, that probably would have resulted in all sorts of misunderstandings. I also think that I was ready to end the conversation, and coming up with an alternative seemed too complicated—I, for one, wouldn't have been able to suggest another idea, being, as I already noted, still relatively new to the area.

§

The man should have mentioned the village's location—that much is obvious to me. He knew the area well, and it should have crossed his mind that I might not be thrilled at the prospect of meeting near a border. Borders and their environs, as everyone knows, are usually teeming with policemen. I have all of my documents in order, and I make sure I keep them with me at all times, just like I've been instructed to do, but I still would rather avoid places where there's a higher chance I will be asked to produce them—train stations, for example. I'm afraid of the look I'll get once it's clear I'm not from here.

THE MAN AND I had known each other
for a month. In that time, we'd already met
up twice. We'd texted for a bit before we
got together for the first time, though not
for too long—a week, at most. I would
have been ready to meet earlier. I even remember saying something to that effect,

very soon after we started writing to each other. He, however, seemed reluctant to do so. He said he would like to learn a few things about me first. (I think he'd had some unpleasant experiences in the past.) I told him he was free to ask me anything he wanted, and that I would answer his questions as truthfully as possible.

§

He must have been satisfied with my answers since, only a few days later, he texted me to ask if I was free the following afternoon—we could get together for a drink if I was. I told him I had nothing planned and that I would be happy to meet up with him. He asked if I had a place in mind—he knew I didn't have access to a car (one of the questions he'd asked me was whether I did) so he was willing to meet wherever was most convenient for me.

§

After thinking about it for a moment, I proposed meeting at a bar in the village I currently live in. It's a place I can reach on foot, so that's often where I end up meeting people. The bar also happens to have a terrace overlooking the sea, and that made it seem like a nice place to have a drink.

THE BAR WASN'T very crowded. I was able to spot the man without much difficulty. It helped that he looked just like his pictures, a bit less tanned, perhaps, but that was it. He waved at me, and as I approached, I noticed that he already had a drink in front of him. The table he had chosen was at the far end of the terrace. I remember that the sea was a bit rough that day. The waves were crashing loudly at the bottom, sending sprays of water into the air behind him.

§

I thought we were just having a drink. At a certain point, however—we'd been at the bar for about an hour—the man asked me what I wanted to do for dinner. Before I could even answer, he proposed that we head to a different village. He said he knew a nice restaurant there, in case I was hungry. He himself was very hungry, having had only a relatively small lunch. We would go in his car. The man said it would be his treat.

§

I agreed to the new plan, even though I wasn't all that hungry. I didn't know that many people at the time, and at one point I had decided I would accept every invitation I received. I was also curious about the restaurant, having been struck by the man's description of it. Among other things, he mentioned that it sat on top of a cliff and that it overlooked a cove on the grounds of a famous castle. I knew which castle he was talking about—not surprisingly, as it is one of the area's most popular tourist attractions. I hadn't visited it yet, but I had seen it a few times, from a distance. The man assured me that the view from the restaurant was nothing short of spectacular. The food, too, was supposed to be very good.

IT WAS STILL early when we got there. Except for a couple sitting at the far end of the main dining room, the restaurant was empty. The man exchanged a few words with the host, who quickly led us to a table by a large window. As we unfolded our napkins, I told the man that he hadn't lied

24

about the view. He smiled, and the two of us spent a moment quietly gazing at the blue waters sparkling in the afternoon sunlight.

§

On our way there, the man warned me that we were headed to a seafood restaurant. Most restaurants of that sort, he said, didn't have a menu. Instead, the different varieties of fish that were on offer that day would be brought to our table. We would then have to look them over and decide which one to get. The man told me I should expect to be shown the whole fish. He wanted me to be prepared—not everyone, he said, was comfortable with that method of ordering.

§

Soon after we sat down, our server appeared. He was carrying a large silver tray, the bottom of which was covered in a thick layer of crushed ice. The fish (six of them) were lying on top, one next to the other. I repeated what I'd told the man in the car, namely that I'd let him order for us both, and not just because I knew almost nothing about fish. Remembering what I'd seen elsewhere, I'd assumed (correctly) that the fish would be huge. As I mentioned earlier, I wasn't very hungry, so in my mind there was no question that we'd be sharing one fish. Since I expected to eat less than half of it, I believed it should be the man who decided which one to get.

§

The man replied that he was fine with that. He then proceeded to inspect each fish carefully. After some time, he pointed to a bream with large eyes and silvery scales, which the server promptly declared to be an excellent choice. The two of them discussed how it should be prepared, and then the server disappeared into the kitchen. A moment later, the man summoned another server and ordered a plate of octopus tartare for us to share. As soon as we were alone again, I told him I wouldn't eat any of it. He asked me, in a slightly mocking tone, if it was for ethical reasons. I replied that it wasn't. I told him I had an aversion to mollusks—flabby organisms without an internal armature, I explained, had always repelled me. Then, trying to change the topic, I asked what he did for a living. That's how I learned that he was an architect.

OUR SECOND MEETING must have taken place a few weeks after that. We met, once again, in the village I currently live in. The man was driving home from an event, a conference he'd been invited to speak at. He'd been there for the last several days, and the two of us had exchanged some messages during that time. Before he left, he texted me to let me know he'd be passing through. He asked if I would like to hang out for a little while—if I wanted to, we could meet at the same bar as the last time, the one with a terrace overlooking the sea. I didn't feel like having a drink, so I suggested we meet for a coffee instead. The man replied that a coffee actually sounded better. He said he was feeling a bit tired after the conference.

§

We agreed to meet in the café in the main square, next to the entrance to the castle. (The village I currently live in also has a castle. It's an important tourist attraction in its own right, even though it's nowhere near as big or as impressive as the one by the restaurant where the man and I went for dinner.) The café was crowded, as it usually is on days when the castle is open to the public. Luckily, the man managed to find an empty table as soon as he arrived.

§

I don't remember much about our conversation, but I do recall that at some point the man took out his phone. He had some pictures from the conference he wanted to show me. Most of them were of his talk. He could be seen standing on a lectern in what looked like an abandoned church. There were people seated all around him, in folding chairs and on the floor. They appeared to be listening attentively to him. Some were even taking notes.

§

After about an hour, the man said that he still had a long drive ahead of him and that it was time for him to leave. I walked him to his car. Before we said goodbye, we both agreed to stay in touch.

I ASSUMED THAT had been it—I
wouldn't have been surprised if we never
spoke again. A few days later, however, I
got a text from him. A good friend of his,
a dancer, was doing a performance that
weekend. The man was wondering if I was

free and if I'd be interested in going with him.

§

I haven't mentioned this yet, but the man lived on the other side of the border, in what is technically a different country. He lived in the capital, in a house he had designed himself. From what I understood, the capital was home to more than half of the country's population. (I expressed my surprise at this at one point, and the man replied that the country was quite small, even by the standards of the region—it didn't have a large population to begin with, and the number of cities was limited to just a few.) Contrary to what I had assumed, though, the performance wouldn't take place in the capital but in a small town by the sea, about an hour's drive away from there. The town, I learned, was on the same bay as the village I currently live in— the man told me that it sat directly across the water from me, at the tip of a peninsula that, on clear days, I should be able to make out in the distance.

§

I'd heard about the town. Only recently, I'd added it to my list of places to visit— several people I'd spoken with had recommended it to me. I told the man I was interested, and we agreed to talk before the weekend. After a busy few days, however, I forgot all about it, at least until he called me on the phone that night. The purpose of that call, in fact, was to come up with a plan.

§

At some point during our conversation, I let the man know that I had an embarrassing confession to make. I told him that, until not very long ago, I had no idea that his country had a coastline. For some reason, I'd always assumed it was land-locked. The man seemed amused. Apparently, it wasn't the first time someone said that to him. Many people were under the same impression—so many, in fact, that the country's tourism board had decided to launch an entire campaign aimed at setting the record straight. The seaside town where the performance would take place, the man said, figured prominently in many of the ads.

§

It's probably unfair of me to blame the man for the fact that we ended up meeting near the border, since it's not as if I played no role in the matter. I knew that the town we were headed to was only an hour's drive from where he lived. Assuming that if he came to pick me up he would have to drive quite a long way, I told him I wouldn't mind meeting him somewhere more convenient, provided I could get there by bus.

It was then that he proposed meeting in that village—which, unbeknownst to me, turned out to be not just close to the border but right next to it. If we met there, he said, he'd be able to hop on and off the freeway easily.

§

The man and the dancer were part of the same social circle. They had a lot of friends in common, many of whom would also be attending the performance. The man made a point of mentioning that a good number of them were artists, no doubt in order to make the trip sound more appealing to me. (He didn't need to do that—I was genuinely interested in the performance, and the town, as I mentioned, was already on my list of places to visit.) I could tell that he really wanted me to come along, and I initially assumed it was because of his friend—the man had mentioned at some point that she was worried not many people would come. However, that turned out not to be the reason, or not the main reason anyway. What the man really wanted to do, I would eventually learn, was to show me a grave.

THE MAN WAS already at the village when I arrived. He'd been there for some time. While I was still on my way, he'd texted me to let me know he didn't have much farther to go and that he'd wait for me at a café. He dropped me a pin—the café, he wrote, was just a few blocks from where I would be getting off. He'd most likely be sitting outside, at one of the tables in front.

§

I was about to cross the street when he saw me. He waved at me and then stood up, waiting for me as I made my way through the tables and greeting me with a hug. He asked me about the bus ride—he wanted to know if it had been okay. I told him I'd almost made a mistake while switching buses halfway through, but that the journey had been fine apart from that. Pointing at an empty coffee cup on the table, he asked if I would like to order anything. I thought about it for a second, but decided not to in the end. He said that in that case we should get going.

§

The man went to pay for his coffee. Before he disappeared through the door, I told him I would wait for him on the sidewalk. I recognized his car right away. It was parked in front of the café. It was an expensive car, with white leather seats and a fancy sound system. I knew the sound system was fancy because the first time we met, on our way to the restaurant, the man had put on a concerto by a well-known composer—as we wound our way along the cliffs, I felt almost as if I were inside the concert hall, sitting a few feet away from the pianist.

§

The man came back out and walked toward the car. I'd been standing by the passenger door, waiting for him. I heard a beep, followed by the soft click of the locks. I opened the passenger door and got in. Immediately after the man started the car, a blast of cold air issued from the vents.

The concerto I mentioned came through the speakers. While fiddling with my seat belt, I jokingly asked him if that was the only thing he ever played. He smiled. Then, reaching toward the screen on the dashboard, he asked if I'd like him to find something else. I told him I was a fan of that concerto and would be perfectly happy listening to it, which he seemed pleased about.

§

Fifteen minutes into our drive, I asked the man if we'd be approaching the border soon—I said I was surprised not to have seen it yet, considering how close it seemed to be when I looked at the map. The man let out a laugh and said we'd already crossed it. We'd actually crossed it a while ago, just a few minutes after we left. It makes sense that I didn't notice since everywhere near the border (this is true even in the village I currently live in) the signs are in more than one language. You can't rely on suddenly not understanding what they say to know that you've crossed into a different country.

IT TOOK US an hour to get to the town. As we drew closer, the man explained that it could have taken us much longer. Even though it was a sunny day, the season hadn't officially started—his fellow citizens, he said, weren't in the habit of heading to the coast just because it was nice out. As a result, there was very little traffic on the road.

§

Something else the man mentioned as we drew closer to the town was that it would be impossible to find parking near the center. This, he explained, was always the case, regardless of whether the season was already underway. We would park, instead, in an area at the top of a hill, where he was sure there'd be a spot.

§

By the time we got out of the car, it was almost one in the afternoon. The performance was supposed to start at two, so we had time for a quick lunch. Luckily for us, the town was relatively small; the man assured me that we were only ten minutes from the promenade. There was a restaurant there that he liked.

§

On our way to the promenade, the man shared several interesting facts about the town. One of them was that it lay near some famous salt pans. The salt from those pans, he said, had at one time been well-known throughout the region. There was even a popular brand of salt named after the town, which I'd probably come across at the supermarket. The pans were no longer active, though, so the salt that was sold under that brand most likely came from somewhere else.

§

The restaurant the man had in mind was closed for renovations, so we ended up at a sandwich shop a few doors down. The place was surprisingly crowded, but we managed to find two seats at the counter by the window. While we were waiting for our food to come out, the man brought up the salt pans again. He said they were an interesting place to walk around, and that we could check them out later if we felt like it, provided there was enough time—he wasn't sure what the plan was for after the performance.

§

As it happened, the salt pans weren't the only thing the town was known for. People, the man said, also visited it because of its picturesque architecture.

DURING OUR MEAL, the man informed me that the performance would take place in an old warehouse by the sea. The building, he explained, dated back to the time when the salt pans were still active—it was there, and in other buildings like it, that the salt used to be stored, before it was packed and shipped. The warehouse had been converted into a performance space only recently. The structures nearby had undergone a similar fate. A large depot next door, for example, had been turned into a small museum.

§

People had already started to gather in front of the warehouse by the time we arrived. Shortly after we joined the line, a young woman came out and announced that the performance would last two hours, but that we were welcome to come and go as we pleased. We were also encouraged to move around the space. The performance would be recorded, however, so we were asked to do our best to stay out of the way of the camera crew.

§

It was dark inside the warehouse. The man and I had to tread very carefully at first. There were four spotlights near the center of the space, but they didn't give off much light. They shone on a cluster of velvet robes, the kind a ballet dancer will wear to keep warm off stage—the man's friend, I would soon learn, had trained as a ballet dancer in her youth. The robes were hanging from the ceiling and appeared to be floating in the air, a few inches above the ground. My first impression was that they were very old. The velvet they were made of looked somewhat faded—threadbare, even.

§

Like most of the other people inside the warehouse, the man and I stationed ourselves alongside one of the walls. We stood there for a while, waiting for the dancer to come out. As it happened, she already had—she'd actually been there all along, standing in the midst of the robes and waiting for everyone to come in. The reason it had been difficult to spot her was that she herself was wearing a robe. But then she started to move. In no time, the robes around her were lightly swaying in the air.

§

We watched as the dancer slowly made her way out from underneath the robes. Once she finally emerged, she stood briefly under the spotlights and then took a few steps forward. I saw that she was cradling a small object in her hands, an old metronome. She knelt down and laid it carefully on the ground, setting it in motion before standing back up and shedding her robe. With the metronome ticking steadily in the background, she proceeded to perform a ballet phrase. She repeated the phrase, but with slight alterations. She continued in this way, the phrase becoming more disjointed each time. Before long, she was rolling and crawling on the ground.

HALF AN HOUR into the performance, the man and I decided to step outside for a moment. Others had already been doing this—there was a small crowd in front of the warehouse when the two of us came out. The man walked toward a group of people standing off to the side. I assumed

51

they were the friends he'd told me about, and that turned out to be correct. The man introduced me to them. One by one, I shook their hands.

§

Some of the man's friends, when they heard where I was living, began to speak to me in the language that is spoken there. I don't really speak that language, but one of the languages I do speak (my native language, in fact) is related to it, so I didn't have much trouble understanding what they were saying. Still, I couldn't have replied to them in that language. I had to do that, instead, in the language in which the man and I had been communicating with each other from the start, which I had reason to assume they also knew—practically everyone in that country, I'd been told, was fluent in it. By contrast, the language that the man and his friends spoke among themselves (their native language, that is) was totally incomprehensible to me. I found it strangely pleasant not to be able to understand a word of what they were saying while we all mingled outside the warehouse.

§

After some time, the man turned toward me. He asked if I would be fine on my own for a minute—he wanted to find out what people were doing once the performance was over. No one he'd asked seemed to know, but he'd just spotted someone who might. He said he'd come back as soon as he had an answer.

§

I told the man I'd be okay by myself and, once he was gone, headed toward a nearby bench—my legs were feeling a bit tired after all that time standing. The man returned a short while later and informed me that, as soon as the performance was over, everyone would be heading to a café in the town's main square. Looking at his watch, he said it would probably be a while before that happened—the performance would be over in an hour, and it would most likely take his friend, the dancer, another hour to be ready to go.

§

The man wasn't quite sure what we should do. He confessed he'd seen enough of the performance, though he would be happy to stick around if I wanted to. I told him I felt the same way; I didn't really need to go back in.

§

The man thought about it for a moment. If I felt like it, he said, we could check out a tourist complex on the edge of town. It was an interesting place, definitely worth a visit. Unfortunately, the salt pans were too far away for us to be able to go there and make it back to the main square on time, especially if we walked around them for a little while, which we would of course want to do. The man said that it was also a little too hot—it might not seem that way to me, but the pans were below sea level, so the temperature there was always higher than it was in the town.

THE MAN HAD achieved some fame as an architect. I learned that after our first meeting. Back home from the restaurant, I decided to look him up, only to discover that he'd designed all kinds of buildings, not only in his own country but across the entire continent. Another thing I learned was that for some time already, he'd also been in charge of a foundation devoted to the preservation of his country's architectural patrimony. That made sense. Based on some of the things he'd said, I could tell that he had a great deal of knowledge about architectural history. Our time at the tourist complex only confirmed that impression.

§

The complex dated from the second half of the twentieth century. It had been built by the leader of the man's old country, which the country we were now in (the country where the man lived) used to be part of, but which had since ceased to exist, having broken up into a number of smaller countries at the end of a long and devastating war. The leader of the man's old country had been born in the area. He was convinced, the man said, that the town, which had fallen on hard times after the closure of the salt pans, could become a popular tourist destination, and not just for the country's citizens. He also thought it could attract people from the neighboring countries, where gambling was still illegal. Indeed, in addition to three hotels and a marina, the complex also included a casino, one of the largest, if not the largest, in the region. The man told me that as a child he'd spent a great deal of time at the complex. His parents had taken the family there on vacation almost every summer.

§

Not long after the end of the war, the one that resulted in the disappearance of the man's old country, the complex was put up for sale. It was acquired by a hotel conglomerate that, saddled with debt, went bankrupt in less than a year. The complex was closed and put up for sale again. It ended up in the hands of a holding company, which also went bankrupt soon after.

A third company bought it, only to go bankrupt, too. It was, the man said, as if the place was cursed.

§

The complex sat abandoned for more than a decade. It seemed as though it would remain in that state forever, but one day the government announced it would take ownership of it. There was talk of reopening it—the idea was to have the students from one of the country's hospitality schools conduct their training there—but that never materialized. Instead, the complex was sold again, this time to a hotel chain known for its meticulous restorations of important architectural landmarks. The man said he'd been involved in the work that was done on the complex, though not in an official capacity—he'd mainly consulted on matters in which his extensive knowledge of architectural history could prove helpful. In his opinion, the hotel chain had done a remarkable job on the restoration. The complex, he said, looked exactly like it used to.

THE TOUR OF the complex took longer than the man said it would. He hadn't been there in a while, and the place turned out to be much bigger than he remembered. I even wondered, at one point, if he had gotten lost. We'd looked at the three hotels (the man had pointed out for

me all of the features that made the buildings interesting from an architectural
standpoint) and were supposed to head to
the casino next, but after going up and
down various stairways and crossing a se-
ries of courtyards, it was clear that we were
getting nowhere near it. The man did his
best to hide his disorientation, but he
wasn't able to fool me. After a while,
clearly frustrated, he suggested that we
start making our way to the main square.
We didn't want to be late—people, he said,
were probably gathering at the café already.

§

Walking down the promenade on our way
to the café, we passed by a kiosk. There was
a folding sign next to it, with pictures of
various desserts, all consisting of some
elaborate combination of ice cream,
whipped cream, and sliced fruit. The
presentation of the desserts was also

elaborate, featuring tiny umbrellas (the kind you often see in tropical drinks) and little palm trees made of foil. I knew we were running late, but I asked the man if it would be okay for me to stop and photograph the sign. The sun had caused the pictures to fade, and some of the colors had changed in ways that made them look very strange. I could imagine someone having a hard time figuring out what it was that they showed.

THE MAN AND I were the last ones to arrive at the café. I recognized most of the people I saw. Some of the faces, however, were new. One of the people I recognized was the dancer. She'd changed out of her costume and was holding a bouquet in her lap.

§

The group was sitting at a large table, with the chairs arranged so that everyone could see the square. This left one side of the table unoccupied. As the last to arrive, the man and I had no choice but to sit at one end, the only place where there was still room. The man sat next to one of his friends, and I, in turn, sat next to him, somewhat off to the edge—it wouldn't have made sense for me to sit next to the man's friend, whom I didn't know. As a result, the man was the only person I could talk to. Before long, though, he was busy talking to his friend. Naturally, he'd switched to the language everyone had been speaking when we were outside the warehouse. Once again, I found it strangely pleasant not to be able to understand a word of what they were saying.

§

A server approached. I asked the man what he was thinking of ordering, and he told me he'd probably have what most people at the table were having, a special cocktail made with schnapps, widely considered to be the national drink. I'm not a big fan of schnapps, but since it was supposed to be the national drink, I decided I might as well give it a try. The man seemed pleased to hear me order one for myself. As soon as the server was gone, he let me know I'd made a good choice. Then he asked me if I was doing okay. I told him I was, and he went back to talking to his friend.

WITH NO ONE to talk to, I was free to direct my attention to the square, where I soon caught sight of a strange scene. A tall figure, dressed in what looked like a chain-mail jumpsuit, quietly approached the statue at the center. A dozen others, all clad in similar outfits, soon followed. Their faces were hidden behind close-fitting masks—also made of chainmail, from what I could tell—so their identities remained a mystery. They gathered at the bottom of the statue and, without saying a word, began to whirl around it. A few of the people in the square turned to look at them. Almost everyone else, though, decided to ignore them.

§

The man and I had encountered one of those figures on our way back from the complex. It happened soon after I had finished photographing the sign by the kiosk. We'd left the promenade and were walking down a narrow street when, upon reaching an intersection crowded with tourists, a shadow swept past us. Everyone fell silent for a moment. The shadow eventually disappeared at the far end of the street, but the sound of clinking metal lingered in the air for a while afterwards. I assumed one of the local teenagers had decided to play a joke on visitors, but that clearly turned out to be wrong.

§

The man caught me staring at the figures in the square. Leaning over, he informed me that I was looking at a performance that had been unfolding since dawn. The friend he'd been speaking with had just shared that with him. There were, in fact, multiple performances taking place in the town that day—the one we'd been to was just one of them. All of the performances were connected to an exhibition at a nearby gallery. At some point, the man said, everyone at the table would be heading there for the opening.

§

Watching the figures move around the statue at the center of the square, I found myself thinking about a story the man had told me while we were at the tourist complex. It involved one of his friends, a woman I'd met at the performance—she'd been outside the warehouse when he and I came out. She was now at the café, though at the far end of the table, sitting next to the dancer. She'd stood out to me at the warehouse because of the bouquet she was carrying, most likely the same one the dancer now held in her lap. The man had introduced us, and the two of us had exchanged a few words. I immediately found myself drawn to her. She seemed very friendly and kind. I said something to that effect while the man and I were touring the complex, and that is how he ended up telling me about her.

THE MAN TOLD me that the woman was an artist. He would have liked to be more specific and say that she was a visual artist, but he wasn't sure if she still identified as one. In any case, she'd had a long and distinguished career. She'd actually achieved a good deal of success along the way. This was primarily the result of some drawings she'd made several years back. The story the man was about to tell me centered, in fact, around those drawings.

§

The woman possessed remarkable artistic abilities. Her technical skills, in particular, were outstanding. Everyone knew that to be the case, but these drawings proved it beyond doubt. The strong political message they conveyed was equally worthy of note, as most of the art from that time was completely lacking in such a message, even though the war, the one the man had mentioned while telling me about the complex and its troubled history, had just come to an end. One would think that the art that is created in the aftermath of a war is bound to convey a strong political message, the man said, but that turned out not to be true in this particular case. The case of the art that was made during the war was different—very different, in fact. Most works from that time definitely conveyed that kind of message. But that changed abruptly once the war ended.

§

The man had no idea why that was. Most likely, everyone just wanted to forget what had happened—including artists, contrary to what one might think. But then one day the woman appeared on the scene, shaking everyone out of their complacency with those drawings. The man said that she couldn't have picked a better time to do that, as critics had already been discussing the need for the kind of art she was making—people, they said, needed to be reminded that art could, and in some cases should, convey a strong political message. The woman's work, however, was well received not just by critics. The general public also liked it. This was strange, to say the least. As the man had just explained, everyone, up to that point, had seemed fine—happy, even—with the state of amnesia the country had slipped into. People must have liked the shock of being woken up from that state, the man said. That was the only explanation he could think of.

§

Of course, one shouldn't underestimate the role played by the woman's remarkable technical skills. The general public tends to favor art that displays superior talent. Critics care about that too, but not as much. When it came to the woman's drawings, the man said, everyone could see that they were the work of a gifted artist, even those who lacked any special knowledge or training in art.

§

The woman became quite successful as a result of those drawings. She ended up making a name for herself, the man said, and a good deal of money as well. As strange as it may sound, the years immediately following the war were a period of great prosperity for his country. (I shouldn't be surprised to hear that, the man said—one could find similar examples throughout history.) A sizable portion of the new wealth flowed into the art sector. In that sense, too, the woman couldn't have picked a better time to appear on the scene.

§

The man was, of course, speaking figuratively, since the woman didn't really choose to appear on the scene at that particular time—she just did, by virtue of her age. She'd finished her studies not long before, so it was naturally time for her to launch her career.

THE WOMAN CONTINUED to make those drawings for a long time. She had no plans to work on anything else. She had plenty of ideas for them and was always finding ways to make them more complex and more technically demanding, so as not to lose interest in them. However, that changed one day. Something happened, the man said. She started to feel trapped. That was how she put it when she spoke to him about it.

§

It was mainly her superior technical skills that she felt trapped by. The woman thought that if her drawings conveyed a strong political message, it was because she had wanted them to do so. All in all, though, she didn't care very much about that aspect of them. Conveying a strong political message had seemed urgent at one point, but years later it no longer did. Often it felt hollow—to her, at least. However, when it came to the high (or, more to the point, the unusually high) level of skill that was in evidence in her drawings, she didn't think that she had much of a choice. She was incapable of drawing in a way that didn't end up calling attention to her abilities. Not that she wanted to show off. She just couldn't help but challenge herself, striving with each new drawing to accomplish something she knew would be exceedingly difficult. It wasn't only a matter of remaining interested in what she was doing. For as long as she could remember, she had found it impossible not to push herself in this way. She liked to test what she was capable of. She liked how that felt. She'd work diligently, refusing to surrender until she achieved her goals, regardless of the problems and the hindrances she encountered along the way. This approach, if one could call it that, would yield stunning results, invariably so, and these drawings were not the exception. That, the man said, was what she one day started to feel trapped by.

§

The woman didn't like feeling that way. She knew she had to do something, but nothing she tried seemed to work. The compulsion to turn every drawing into a test was too deeply ingrained. It kept reasserting itself, even when she made an effort to proceed differently. Eventually, she decided it would be good for her to take a break. A pause was in order—a temporary pause, obviously: she had no reason to think otherwise. That, at least, was what she told herself. Deep down, she knew she might have to stop drawing for good. Of course, that wouldn't be enough—she knew that, too. For it wouldn't solve the problem posed by the drawings that were already in existence, which, as she liked to say, she had since grown to hate, finding it difficult not to see, in each, a damning testament to her compulsion.

§

Those she discussed this with often asked her if she would like to renounce the work she had done up to that point. The man himself had asked her that once. After thinking about it for a moment, the woman shook her head. She said she'd never liked that word. Not only was it too religious for her taste, too close to the idea of sacrifice. It could also give people the idea that she had an exaggerated sense of her own importance—arrogance, she explained, was something she'd always found repellent. Not to mention that she would like to go further than that. Disowning the work she'd done up to that point—effectively what renouncing it would amount to—didn't seem to be enough. She actually wished she'd never made those drawings. She'd be happy if they didn't exist. What she wanted, she said, was to retract them. That seemed to her to be the right thing to do, mainly because she would actually be doing something, which wasn't necessarily the case if she were simply to renounce them—a shift in how she felt about them, a refusal to stand by them and to be associated with them, was all that would take. Retracting them would be a very different thing. In her mind, the work she'd done up to that point constituted a statement of sorts, one she had now decided to withdraw. However, a retraction is itself, by definition, a statement. Withdrawing the statement she'd made would require her to issue a new statement—to make another work, that is. She liked that. Her decision to stop drawing, she confessed to the man, had stirred up some fears. She wondered if, having stopped, she'd find herself unable to do anything, not just drawing, ever again. In choosing a course of action that required her to do something, she was forcing herself to confront those fears head-on.

THE WOMAN DIDN'T know what to do. It wasn't clear to her what form her retraction should take. She had a number of ideas, but she couldn't decide which one to pursue. She was afraid of making a mistake, as there was no guarantee that whatever seemed right to her at that moment wouldn't end up being something she would, down the line, want to retract.

§

She agonized over all of this for a while, but then one day it dawned on her that, even if she ended up making a mistake, she at least would have done something different than what she normally did, since that mistake would be the result of a choice, whereas previously she had acted out of habit—it was impossible for her not to do what she did, which was to challenge herself compulsively. She'd never really questioned why she would challenge herself in that way and whether she even wanted to, and that was how she'd ended up feeling trapped.

§

It helped her to understand this, the man said. One of the ideas she'd been considering seemed especially promising. Now she felt ready to take action. The very next day, she went to see a lawyer. With his help, she drafted a notice that formally declared her intention to retract the work she'd done up to that point. After that, she gathered all of the drawings she'd ever made (or as many of them as she was able to track down) and proceeded to erase them one by one. It wasn't an easy task, but she dedicated herself to it, working every day almost without pause. Once she started, she wouldn't stop, at least not until it became physically impossible for her to continue.

§

Three months later, she was done. But that wasn't the end of it. The erased drawings (blank sheets of paper, essentially) were rolled up and placed inside cardboard shipping tubes. She then had a wooden crate built inside her studio, large enough to accommodate a few people—she had a door installed on it for that purpose. The crate, shaped like a cube, was painted black on the outside, with a special kind of paint that gave the exterior walls the appearance of polished marble. It exuded a solemn, almost reverent aura. ('The little Kaaba,' the man had once called it, much to the woman's delight.) The interior, however—and this applied not only to the walls, but also to the floor and the ceiling—was painted white, a pristine white, so that when you went in, you almost felt as if you had stepped into a small gallery. Except that nothing was hanging on the walls—all you saw were the cardboard tubes, stacked in neat piles on the floor.

§

The woman invited her friends over to her studio one evening, for a party. There were drinks and hors d'oeuvres, and anyone who wished to enter the crate was encouraged to do so. She placed copies of the legal notice on a small pedestal by the door. The original was in a safe-deposit box. The woman had put it there, in accordance with the lawyer's instructions.

§

The party lasted well into the night. The following morning, the door to the crate was nailed shut. The crate was then loaded onto a truck. It was a complicated operation. The crate ended up being too large to fit through the door of the woman's studio, even though she'd been very clear with her instructions and, once the job was finished, had checked that the measurements were correct. In the end, the door had to be removed. Part of an adjoining wall, too, had to be torn down.

§

The woman had arranged for the crate to be driven to the country's main port. She'd hired a boat, which would take the crate somewhere far out to sea. At a specific time, the crate would be dropped in the water. The idea, the man said, was for it to sink to the bottom.

THE WOMAN ASKED the man to accompany her to the port. It made sense for her to do that, the man said—she was about to take a massive step and would rather not be alone. Obviously, he agreed. He drove them both in his car, behind the truck with the crate. Three hours later, they arrived at the port. The trip shouldn't have taken that long—I knew how small the country was—but the route led through a mountain pass, and after what happened in the woman's studio, the truck driver decided to exercise great caution. He stopped before every tunnel, to double-check that the crate wasn't too wide and the truck would make it through.

§

The crate had to be loaded onto the boat with a forklift. The woman had hired one in advance, and the man in charge of operating it was already at the dock when they arrived. So was the boat captain. Both seemed impatient—understandably, as the two of them had been waiting for hours.

§

It took some time for the crate to be correctly attached. It kept tipping to one side, no one could figure out why. The issue was eventually resolved. But then, as soon as the crate was raised, a loud noise filled the air. The bottom, apparently, was starting to crack open. The forklift operator was wearing earplugs so he didn't hear anything—the woman had to run toward him and wave her arms to get his attention. She explained what was happening, and he immediately lowered the crate back onto the truck.

§

The woman and the forklift operator took a moment to discuss what they should do next. The crack looked serious, but the crane operator insisted that he could load the crate onto the boat quickly, before the bottom gave out. The boat captain, however, was beginning to feel apprehensive. He'd been standing next to the dock, smoking and watching the whole operation unfold with a skeptical look on his face. While the woman and the forklift operator were talking, he stepped forward to announce that he didn't want the crate on his boat anymore. The woman protested. She reminded him that they had an agreement and that she'd already paid him, but the captain wouldn't budge. He was convinced that something bad would happen if he allowed the crate onto his boat. The woman begged him. She told him that she'd made no other plans, assuming it would all be very straightforward. She really didn't want the crate to sit by the dock while she figured out what to do with it. The captain kept refusing, and that was when the truck driver intervened. He told the woman about a storage facility nearby. He had an arrangement with the owner and would be happy to drive the crate there at no extra cost. At the man's recommendation, the woman decided to accept his offer.

THE PERFORMANCE continued to unfold in the square. The masked figures, however, were no longer whirling around the statue; they'd scattered in different directions and were now tiptoeing their way through the crowd. The drinks the man and I had ordered still hadn't arrived. We'd been waiting quite a while, so I thought I should say something. Just then, the server appeared. He placed the drinks in front of us and, pressing his tray flat against his chest, exchanged a few words with the man. I couldn't understand what he was saying, but I assumed he was apologizing for the delay.

§

All of a sudden, the sound of bells filled the square. I looked behind me, at the church on the far end. A large group had congregated on the front steps, in front of a tour guide who, while speaking, kept gesturing toward the belfry and the spire above. I turned around and saw a couple walk by. The man was wearing a suit; the woman, in a short dress and extremely high heels, was holding on to his arm. One of the masked figures decided to follow them. Soon, it started dancing around them, at times forcing them to slow down. They tried to ignore it. The figure had suddenly turned them into the center of attention, which they clearly didn't like—both seemed embarrassed, especially the woman, who was struggling with her heels and was trying hard not to trip on the square's cobblestone surface. As I watched them, I wondered if they were on their way to the opening at the nearby gallery, the one everyone at the café would be heading to eventually.

§

Although I'd been happy quietly going over the story the man had told me, I wouldn't have minded joining one of the conversations taking place at the table. I already knew, based on what the man had said to me on the phone, that a good number of the people sitting there were artists. Possibly, some of them were famous, just like the man—I remember thinking I might even know their work. On our way to the café, the man had told me that they were all about the same age as he was and that they had also lived through the war, the one he'd mentioned while we were at the complex. In the years since, a number of them had gone on to become directors of cultural institutions and professors. Not the woman, though—the man said she'd never been anything other than an artist.

§

More than anyone else at the table, it was the woman I would have liked to talk to. For that, though, I would have to wait a little. It happened very suddenly. The band at the opening started playing. (The gallery wasn't far away, so we could hear the music from the café.) The moment the notes of a saxophone drifted over into the square, everyone got up from their chairs. Later I'd learn why they seemed to be in such a hurry: some of them (those who, according to the man, had gone on to become

directors of cultural institutions and professors) were in town that day in an official
capacity; they'd traveled there not only to
attend the dancer's performance—or any
of the other performances, for that matter.
Their presence was required at the opening; a couple of them, the man said, were
even expected to give speeches. The others
were going with them for moral support.

THE MAN AND I ended up staying behind. So did the woman and the dancer.
The four of us would join the others at the
opening, but only after we had a chance to
talk among ourselves for a little while. We
hadn't been able to do that yet, due to the
way the chairs had been arranged at the

table. The woman and the dancer wanted to talk to the man, whom they hadn't seen in a while, though it was clear that they also wanted to talk to me. Naturally, they were curious to learn more about the stranger their friend had brought along.

§

The woman and the dancer stood up. They grabbed their drinks and, dragging their chairs in tow, made their way over to where the man and I were sitting. Soon, the four of us were laughing, and not only because of the terrible noise the chairs made as they scraped the ground. In addition to her drink, the dancer also had to juggle the bouquet she had been carrying in her lap, which resulted in some funny movements on her part.

§

The four of us ended up forming a small circle. However, just as we were getting ready to start talking, the server approached. The woman exchanged a few words with him, and it wasn't long before things grew heated. The man joined in. I didn't know what any of them were saying, on account of the language barrier, so I was grateful when the dancer decided to interpret for me. She explained that the others had left without paying.

§

It was outrageous, the dancer said, with an expression of amusement on her face. Artists just won't grow up. They'll continue to behave like they did when they were students, no matter how old they are and no matter their financial situation, which, for many who'd been sitting at the table with us, was a far cry from what it was in those days. They were all poor back then, the dancer said, so it was understandable if they left without paying—they used to do that constantly. However, a lot of time had passed since then. A good number of them had gone on to find success and were now doing quite well for themselves. Some, as the man might have told me, were now directors of cultural institutions and professors. The dancer rolled her eyes, took a sip of her drink, and smiled.

§

The man and the woman continued to argue with the server. After a while, the woman shook her head, let out a big sigh, and then began to rummage through her purse. She took out her wallet and handed the server a card. The server turned around and ran to a podium at the edge of the terrace. He came back with the contact reader. The woman tapped her card, and the four of us waited in silence for the payment to go through.

§

I looked at the square. The masked figures continued to move around it. Once again, they were whirling, this time with their arms wide open. It took me a little while, but I eventually realized they were dancing to the music coming from the opening at the gallery.

THE SERVER HANDED the woman the receipt and left. The four of us were finally able to talk. At first, the conversation centered on the dancer's performance. I'd told the man, as soon as we were outside the warehouse, that I'd been struck by the music that started playing after she had been rolling on the ground for a while. I'd asked him if he knew what it was, but he said he had no idea. We both agreed that it sounded like the music you would hear in a film. The man said he was thinking, specifically, about a film set in a small seaside town, similar to the one we were in. He didn't have a particular film in mind—he wasn't sure that the film he was thinking about even existed. It was, he said, more of an idea.

§

The music had made me think about a soft-porn film from the seventies. Unlike the man, though, I did have a specific film in mind, one I'd seen on TV as a child. It had made a big impression on me, for obvious reasons, so I had no trouble remembering the title. I shared all of this with everyone, and the dancer told me I'd guessed correctly. She was impressed. No one else had been able to identify the music with such precision. She told me the composer's name, but it didn't sound familiar. She said he'd been active at a certain time and had worked with several directors. She mentioned other films, but none of the titles rang a bell.

§

The woman asked me how I'd liked the complex. She knew the man and I had been there—the man had told her we'd be heading that way before we left the warehouse. I said I had enjoyed the tour, after which the man repeated a few of the things he'd told me while we were there, about the buildings and the choices the architects in charge of the restoration had made. The woman and the dancer sipped their drinks as he spoke. Every so often, they gave a nod. It was their way of signaling their interest in what he was saying.

§

It turned out that, like the man, the woman and the dancer had also stayed at the complex when they were young. Both of them said they had very fond memories of the place. Turning to the man, the woman said that he probably did as well. The man, however, didn't say anything. He just smiled and looked down. In response, the woman placed her hand on top of his wrist. She then looked at me and asked me if it was true that I was also an artist.

§

The man hadn't mentioned any specific memories while we were at the complex. I was almost expecting him to, especially since, as he'd told me, his parents had taken the family there on vacation almost every summer. While we were wandering around the different buildings, though, his attention had been focused almost exclusively on the story he was telling me, the story about the woman and her drawings. He did interrupt the story a few times, but it was to point out the buildings' most salient features.

§

I told the woman I was also an artist. She asked me what I did exactly, and I gave her the answer I like to give whenever someone asks me that. It sounded false, as it always has, but for different reasons: I really wasn't doing any of the things I mentioned anymore. I actually hadn't done anything for a while, so it felt to me as if I were speaking not about me but about someone else, someone I'd known a long time ago but had since become estranged from.

§

Still, I was glad that she asked, as it allowed me to ask her the same question in return and, once I'd done that, to bring up the story of her drawings. I wasn't sure how she would react—I was afraid she'd be annoyed to learn I knew all about them. Instead, she seemed happy. She did slap the man's wrist, as if to reprimand him for the part he'd played in that, but it was all clearly in jest. The slap, I couldn't help but notice, landed right where she'd placed her hand before, when she told the man that he probably had fond memories of the complex too.

THE CRATE WITH her drawings, the woman said, was still at the storage facility. So even though it hadn't ended up at the bottom of the sea, the result was more or less the same. In the beginning, the thought of it sitting there had caused her great distress, but then she realized she didn't have to feel that way. The crate, after all, didn't contain all of the drawings she'd ever made, but only those she'd been able to take possession of. Many of those drawings were owned by friends and acquaintances whom she'd had no trouble convincing that they should be returned to her. The man and the dancer, for example, had agreed to part with the ones they owned—reluctantly, they were both quick to point out, since those works had hung in their homes for a long time. But they understood, and were happy to help their friend with something that, as she'd explained to them, she had no choice but to do.

§

A good number of drawings, however, had been acquired by museums, and the protocols in place didn't allow for them to be returned to her. Luckily, she was friends with most of the people in charge of those institutions—one of them had in fact been sitting with us at the café, and was probably giving a speech at the opening as we spoke. It took some effort, but she eventually got them to agree never to display them again. Private collectors proved more challenging to deal with—they grew attached to the drawings in their possession, some of them to an extreme degree. But the woman wasn't too concerned about them, since most kept the bulk of the art they owned in remote storage facilities, not unlike the one where her crate was now sitting.

§

Of course, the woman hadn't been able to track down every single drawing. Some had passed hands too many times and, at one point or another, had been sold to buyers who wished to remain anonymous. Others had been given away as gifts, so their trail had been lost. There were also drawings whose existence she'd simply forgotten about. (Something like that could happen—more than once, she'd stumbled upon one she didn't remember making.) There was no way for her to know the exact number of those, but she'd decided not to give that too much thought—the legal notice she'd drafted contained a clause dealing specifically with the issue of any drawings she might not, for whatever reason, be able to retrieve. Still, whenever one surfaced, she found herself feeling quite annoyed. More often than not, somebody would be trying to sell it. She would do what she could to get it back—she'd gone so far as to buy several of them herself—but she wasn't always successful. Considering how she felt, the fact that the crate was sitting at a storage facility didn't seem so bad after all. She'd come to think that it would have been premature to drop it in the middle of the sea the way she had originally intended to.

§

The woman would have liked to accomplish what she'd set out to do. But that didn't seem meant to be. The retraction she'd envisioned would have to be put on hold. She wasn't giving up. She had every intention of finishing what she'd started. So she believed at first—as time went on, though, she was forced to accept that she never might. It actually felt to her as if she shouldn't—she'd begun to think that, if she kept insisting, she could end up attracting some misfortune. (She didn't consider herself a superstitious person, but she clearly acted like one in this case.) At any rate, it was now a question of doing something else entirely. This seemed not only necessary, but urgent. Her fear that, having stopped making those drawings, she might not be able to do anything ever again was slowly creeping back into her mind. But as to what that should be, she

didn't know. Once again, she found herself
at a loss.

§

Pointing to the man, the woman said that
she might never have found a way out of
her predicament if it hadn't been for him.
I wasn't sure what she meant, so I turned
to the man, hoping he would clarify things
for me. The man gave a smile and then
looked inquiringly at the woman. He was
asking her if it would be okay for him to
take over. The woman returned his smile,
extending her hand out and then bowing
to him. It was a deliberately theatrical ges-
ture, the purpose of which was to let the
man know that he now had the floor to
himself.

EVERY TWO YEARS, the man said, the foundation he presided over would award a prize to a talented young architect. To raise money for the prize, the foundation organized an art auction, a high-profile event that never failed to attract a great deal of publicity. Back then, the man, who had been on the foundation's board for several years, had just been elected president. It seemed like the right time to do something different, as had been his wish for a while.

§

The auction, the man said, had always been a private event. He, however, wanted it to be open to everyone. Of course, for that to make sense, the items that were up for auction would need to be more affordable than those that were typically featured—works of art, the man said, tend not to be cheap. As it happened, the architect after whom the foundation was named had also been a furniture designer. Like many architects, he had a very specific vision for the spaces he created; he wanted them to look a certain way, and had very strict requirements for how they should be furnished. He'd designed a chair that, in his mind, fit that vision well, and which had since become quite famous—it was, in fact, the first thing most people thought of when they heard his name. (The man described the chair for me, and the woman and the dancer assured me I had seen it—they claimed it was everywhere. It took some time for me to picture it in my mind, but once I did, I realized they were right.) The man decided that the auction would be devoted exclusively to chairs. This, he thought, would not only appeal to a larger public; it would also be a fitting homage to the architect after whom the foundation was named, since it was, after all, a chair, rather than the buildings he'd designed, that had secured his place in the public imagination.

§

The chairs up for sale wouldn't be collectors' items, of the kind one might find in a high-end vintage furniture store. Instead, they'd be created exclusively for the event.

The man (or the foundation, to be precise) would invite a select group of architects, furniture designers, and artists to design one. Initially, the man had thought that the group should only include architects and furniture designers. That made sense to him, considering both the nature of what was to be auctioned and the specific background of the architect after whom the foundation was named. (Not to mention that, until then, the auction had been exclusively an art auction and the whole point was to do something different— some might have argued, not without reason, that a chair designed by an artist was technically a work of art.) In the end, though, the man decided to include artists as well. The chairs they created, he believed, were bound to be interesting. So would those created by the architects and the furniture designers he invited, of course, but artists were more likely to come up with some unconventional ideas. In the case of an event that never failed to attract a good deal of publicity, that was obviously not a bad thing. In addition, people were more likely to pay more for a chair designed by an artist than for one designed by an architect or a furniture designer. Having a few expensive items, the man thought, wouldn't seriously compromise his vision for the auction. The whole purpose of the event, he said, was to raise money—one couldn't simply ignore that fact.

THE WOMAN WAS invited to create a chair for the auction. She was an important artist, the man said, so there was no way she wasn't going to be included. (Upon hearing this, the woman pressed her hand against her chest, lowering her head slightly and smiling gently at the man.) It was true that at the time she didn't have a clear sense of what direction her work would take, but that wasn't a valid reason to exclude her. The woman, however, was reluctant to accept. There was nothing surprising about this, given the fact that she'd never designed a piece of furniture. In fact, she'd never come up with anything that served any kind of function. For longer than she cared to remember, she'd only made those drawings.

§

In the end, the man was able to persuade her. The woman, however, failed to come up with an interesting concept, or at least so she thought—nothing satisfied her fully. She decided to withdraw from the auction, and was in fact on the verge of doing so—she'd already dialed the man's number—when she suddenly had an idea. It felt right from the start. She experienced no hesitation at all. It hadn't been like that with the various ideas she'd entertained more recently, as she tried to determine what she should do next, so this almost felt new to her. She'd come to expect whatever certainty and enthusiasm she felt at the beginning to abruptly wane—for no apparent reason, as far as she could tell—and all sorts of doubts to creep up before long. But this time it wasn't like that. She couldn't quite put her finger on why.

§

The man had been right to assume that artists would come up with some unconventional ideas. This held true, in particular, for the woman's contribution. She'd realized that creating a chair had never been of any interest to her. She'd rather grab an already existing chair (any ordinary chair would do) and use it to create an experience. It was all supposed to be very straightforward. She would place a chair somewhere. Then, she would have someone sit on it. That was basically it—or at least it was at the very beginning, when the idea first flickered through her mind. It got slightly more complicated as she revised it to involve two chairs—and two people—instead of one, having understood that, when it came to the experience she wanted to create, one person alone wouldn't be enough. Two people would have to sit together for that. (Using three chairs—and having three people sit together—was out of the question. As she explained to the man, it went against what she had in mind, and it could result in people making all sorts of associations she would rather avoid.)

§

An experience isn't an object, the man said. The one the woman wanted to create needed to be delimited in some way—she was convinced about that. People wouldn't bid on it otherwise. They wouldn't feel that they'd be getting something tangible if they won. The easiest way to achieve that was to assign the experience a specific duration. The woman decided that an hour would be good—it seemed like enough time for something to happen. Because that was, ultimately, what this was all about: to make it possible for something to happen. It was that possibility, in fact, that was up for sale, so said the entry devoted to the woman's contribution in the program for the auction.

THE MAN TURNED toward the woman and asked her if she would like to take over from him. He said she probably should, as it was really her story to tell, not his. The woman replied that he'd been doing a good job so far and that she didn't mind if he continued. The man insisted, however, and she eventually agreed.

§

Where she placed the chairs, the woman said, was obviously crucial. Whatever ended up happening could vary widely depending on that. She considered various options. She actually went all over the country in search of the perfect spot. Eventually, she decided in favor of an abandoned quarry. It might not have seemed like the ideal location—in addition to being a bit remote, the quarry was also somewhat difficult to access—but that was the whole point. She didn't want there to be any disruptions.

§

The woman visited the quarry a few times. On each of those visits, she wandered around the place for hours, climbing up

and down the slabs of fallen rock and following the narrow paths that wound their
way through the various pits. One day, she
came upon a ledge, not far from the top of
the central pit. It was a secluded spot, with
a nice view of the surrounding hills—just
what she'd been looking for. The woman
carried the chairs up there and placed them
near the edge, one next to the other.

§

From the start, it had been clear to the
woman that the chairs shouldn't face each
other. As she explained, she wanted to pre-
vent those who sat in them from becoming
lost in each other's presence. It was important, she said, that they didn't forget
where they were.

§

I could tell, from the silence that followed,
that the quarry possessed a special

significance. I don't know why, but I suspected that the war, the one I kept hearing about, had something to do with it. I would have liked to know for sure, but it didn't feel like the right time to ask. I decided I would ask the man later, but of course I forgot to do so. That is not surprising, given what ended up happening.

IT WAS THE woman's chairs that ended up fetching the most money. To her surprise, a bidding war ensued as soon as the lot was introduced. The identity of the winner, however, was never revealed, not even after the gavel dropped and everyone started clapping. The buyer, people were told, wished to remain anonymous.

§

The woman asked me if I'd already guessed who that was. I told her I had no idea and looked, rather helplessly, at the dancer—she'd come to my aid before, so I probably hoped she would once again take pity on me. The dancer, however, didn't say anything. She just took a sip of her drink and winked at me. I turned toward the man, who blushed in response.

§

The woman said she'd been genuinely surprised. The man had been the one to deliver the news to her—he was the head of the foundation, after all—and though at first she didn't believe him and thought he must be joking, she quickly realized he was being serious. But that was all beside the point. In the end, she couldn't have been more delighted.

THE QUARRY LAY in the midst of a forest that stretched over a large plateau. Scattered nearby were a number of small villages, most of which, like the quarry, had been abandoned a long time ago. The woman and the man had arranged to meet outside one of them, next to an old access road that trucks had once used to haul out the rock. She didn't know the identity of the man's guest. He hadn't told her who it was—it hadn't seemed to her as if he wanted to—and although she was curious, she had decided not to ask him.

§

The roads that led through the forest could be confusing to navigate, and the villages all looked very similar. Not surprisingly, the man got lost along the way. He arrived at the spot where he and the woman were supposed to meet much later than planned. He got out of the car. The woman, who had parked by the side of the road, waited for a while for the passenger door to open. But it never did. The man had come alone.

§

The woman hadn't been expecting that. Still, she decided not to say anything. The two of them walked quietly down the access road. Fifteen minutes later, they reached the quarry's central pit. The ledge where the woman had placed the chairs was at the end of a steep path that climbed up one of the side walls.

§

The sun was already low in the sky by the time they reached the top. The original plan was for it to start setting at the end of the hour that the man and whoever he brought with him were meant to sit there. But since the man had arrived so late, it ended up setting much earlier than that. The woman had to bring a flashlight with her when, an hour later, she came to get him.

§

The woman placed her hand on the man's wrist, just like she'd done before. She was silent for a while. Then she told the man that he hadn't really been at the quarry by himself.

§

I remember feeling slightly embarrassed, as if I'd witnessed something I shouldn't have. My instinct, once again, was to look at the dancer. She gave me a faint smile—I sensed a tinge of sadness in it—and then looked at the man. I did the same. With all eyes now on him, the man looked down. He, too, seemed embarrassed. In the silence that followed, the woman gripped his palm and squeezed it lightly a few times. With each squeeze, the man gave a nod.

THE WOMAN AND the dancer ex-
changed glances. We'd all been silent since
the woman last spoke, and the man continued to look down. The dancer pointed to
her watch. The woman nodded quietly in
response. It seemed as though she was
about to say something, but then the man

looked up. He appeared somewhat dazed, as if he'd just awakened. He smiled at the three of us, and the woman said that it was probably time to head to the opening. People must be wondering where we were.

§

The four of us stood up. The woman and the dancer started gathering their things. I gave a look around me. The square was less crowded than it had been earlier. The masked figures appeared to have vanished—they were nowhere to be seen. After a moment, though, I realized they were still there, lying at the feet of the statue. They seemed to be sleeping—their bodies, at least, were still, and they were breathing with a slow and steady rhythm.

§

The woman asked the man if he and I were coming to the opening. I assumed we were, but the man looked at me, as if to ask whether I felt like it. I shrugged—I didn't particularly want to go, but I also didn't mind if we did. The man didn't seem to feel strongly about it either. Eventually, he said it was getting late (I, especially, had a long journey ahead of me) and that we should probably start heading back instead.

§

The four of us said goodbye. The woman and the dancer remarked that it had been a pleasure to meet me and that they hoped to see me again. As soon as they were gone, the man and I began to make our way back to his car. We left the square through an alley beside the church. Soon, we were climbing up a winding street. We were both silent the whole time—the street was quite steep, and I, for one, felt a bit short of breath.

IT WAS VERY quiet at the top, in stark contrast to the square. Now and then, I could hear a flock of seagulls calling in the distance, along with the voices of people who had come out to their balconies to enjoy what remained of the afternoon. The streets were wider, too—the one we were walking down certainly was—with clear views of the sky. Before long, the man came to a stop. So did I, only to realize that we were standing in front of a cemetery.

§

A staircase led to a stone archway with a large iron gate. There was an inscription at the top, in Latin. I asked the man if he knew what it said, and he replied that although he'd studied Latin in high school, he had since forgotten most of it. He read the words aloud and then translated them for me. It was something having to do with the resurrection of the dead. '*Il senso lor m'è duro*,' I said, half-jokingly. I wondered if he would understand what I'd meant by that. Judging by the knowing smile he gave me, I would say that he did.

§

The gate was open. The man asked me if I would like to go in. I said I did, even though it felt as if I didn't have much of a choice. I also felt, as the two of us walked toward the gate, that he knew the place well.

§

As we made our way back from the square, I had found myself returning to the image of the man sitting next to an empty chair at the top of an abandoned quarry. I could picture him clearly, a silent figure gradually fading away in the gathering darkness. I felt almost as if I'd been there, standing a few steps behind him, and the moment was an actual memory rather than something I was imagining. My mood had started to darken, no doubt as a result of that. Going into the cemetery, I thought, would only make things worse. I recall being suddenly overcome by a strong desire to be by myself. I realized I'd spent the whole day listening to other people, first to the man and then to the woman. While I did that, something had been building inside of me, a vague feeling of unease, which I'd so far managed to keep at bay. I assumed it would fade away on its own, but it didn't. As the man and I crossed the gate, I understood that it wasn't just the strain of the climb that was making it hard for me to breathe. That feeling was also to blame. I didn't know what to make of it. It seemed to me I should regard it as a premonition of sorts, even though I wasn't actually in need of a warning: I'd known, for a while already, that this moment was coming. Now that it had come, though, everything about it struck me as strange. I suddenly had no idea what I was doing in that town, in a country on the other side of a border I had crossed without noticing, walking into a cemetery with a man I barely knew. It dawned on me that I actually didn't know who this man was—the little I knew about him had made it seem as if I did, but it was so little that it might as well have been nothing. But then neither, for that matter, did I know who I was—and that was part of the strangeness of the moment, too. I knew I was someone, but I really didn't know much more beyond that. I felt hollow, devoid of substance, like an apparition, almost. And even though I knew where I was, I felt like I couldn't have explained what I was doing there, in that cemetery and in that town, and also in that country and in that part of the world, among people who spoke to one another in a language I didn't understand or speak, and whose first impulse, upon learning where I was living, was to speak to me in a language I understood but couldn't speak, making it necessary for me, and for them, to resort, in order to communicate, to a language we could both understand and speak, but which remained, fundamentally, foreign to us all.

THE CEMETERY, THE man said, was one of the oldest in the region. I wasn't surprised to learn that; more than a few of the graves we passed looked like they were centuries old. I followed the man past a large columbarium and a row of mausoleums and then down a gravel path lined on both sides with tall cypress trees. As we were nearing the end of the path, the man came to a stop in front of a rectangular granite stone. It lay flat on the ground, rising only a few inches above the surface. A metal plaque at the center showed a name and two dates.

§

The man knelt down, pausing briefly before brushing off the dead leaves piled on top. Once he was done, he got back to his feet and stared at the grave in silence. I don't know why, but I assumed he would start speaking soon. I knew he would be doing that eventually, and I'd been dreading the effect that his words would have on my mood—which, as I mentioned earlier, had darkened considerably since we left the square—so it's possible that a part of me wanted the whole thing to be over quickly, so that we could head back and I could finally be by myself, as was my wish. The man, however, continued to stand quietly in front of the grave, and it would be a while before he opened his mouth.

§

The grave, he said, belonged to someone he'd been very close to in his youth. They'd met at a party a friend threw—I might remember her, she'd actually been at the performance, though not at the café; the man had exchanged a few words with her as we were coming out of the ware-house. Someone brought him along and introduced him to the man. Soon, the two of them started talking. He told the man he'd grown up in a small village in the countryside, but that like almost everyone his age he'd left immediately after he was done with high school. He'd moved to the capital, where he'd been living ever since. He'd always been interested in theater and had spent a few years training as an actor. Eventually, he enrolled at the university, initially with the intention of studying law, but he ended up majoring in philosophy—ancient philosophy, the man said, he was working on his thesis at the time. He never finished that thesis (the man could no longer remember what it was about) since at one point—this was just a few months after they met—he decided to drop out of school. He stopped acting too. He'd been in a few plays in the time the man had known him, but soon after he abandoned his studies he also stopped auditioning for parts. When asked why he'd done that, he would say he had always considered himself an artist and that it was time for him to take that seriously. He wanted that to be his focus. Anything else, he said, would be a distraction.

§

The man introduced him to his friends. Most of them, as I already knew, were artists, so they got along well with him. At the same time, he remained somewhat of a mystery to everyone, the man included. Once, in the course of one of their conversations, he'd told the man that he had a clear idea of the kind of work he wanted to do as an artist, a vision of sorts. He didn't feel ready to execute it, though. He could tell that he wasn't prepared enough. His life had just begun, so he still had a lot to learn, a lot to experience. Shortly after that conversation, he began to disappear, often for long periods. He wouldn't tell anyone that he was going to disappear; he just did. All of a sudden he wasn't around anymore. No one knew what he was up to during that time, or his whereabouts. The man and his friends often wondered if he was even in the capital. For all they knew, he could be hiding in some remote neighborhood, living like a hermit—they all imagined him doing something like that, for some reason—but he could also be somewhere far away, in a different city, maybe in a different country. He didn't communicate with anyone while he was gone, so there really was no way for them to know.

§

Then, one day, he would return. Months could have gone by, but he'd show up at one of the places where they liked to hang out, greeting everyone as if he'd seen them the day before. He never said much about what he'd been doing; he just said he'd been busy. He wouldn't elaborate on that, and no one ever asked him to. They all felt that it wouldn't be appropriate, that he'd already said as much as he was willing to say.

HE'D BE GONE for long periods, the man said, so the way he would have changed during that time would be quite obvious to everyone. (The man and his friends were of course changing too, but that wasn't so apparent to them since they saw each other regularly.) The changes were most apparent on a physical level. Each time he came back, he looked noticeably thinner. He'd always been thin—he had a reputation for eating very little. Everyone, including the man, had remarked upon that. They were all students back then, so none of them had any money. They spent most of what they had on alcohol, and ate very poorly as a result. He, however, had always seemed okay with that. He never complained about being hungry, unlike the rest of them. Even when someone had a bit of extra money and decided to treat the group to a big feast, he would eat sparingly, in stark contrast to the others, who didn't hesitate to gorge themselves. Still, the change was too obvious to go unnoticed. It was clear he'd lost weight, as if he'd been fasting the whole time he was gone.

§

He was also changing in other ways, the man said, much more difficult to ascertain. He seemed more detached, a little dissociated, even—when you talked to him, you got the impression that he wasn't fully there. He didn't mind when someone pointed that out to him—he actually liked it, just as he liked it when someone commented on the changes in his physical appearance. As he told the man, it made him feel that what he'd been doing was having an effect—on him, of course, but also on others. They'd noticed a shift and were curious about the reasons for it. That, he said, was an effect unto itself.

§

The world around them was changing, too. The first signs of what was to come had surfaced shortly after they met. Most people missed them, though. Signs can be hard to identify in the moment—things seem obvious to us only in hindsight. But it could be that people simply didn't want to see them. At a certain point, however, the situation began to deteriorate in very obvious ways. The news, on television and in the newspaper, was far from uplifting. It was around that time that they started seeing him even less. Not only would he disappear for longer periods, but once he was back, he would rarely spend time with them. They found out he was back only because someone had run into him on the street. Eventually, they lost track of him. One day he disappeared, just like he always did, and when, after a while, someone asked about him, they all looked at each other and realized that they didn't remember when they'd last seen him. They'd almost forgotten about him.

§

It made sense, the man said. The war had just broken out. It was, understandably, the only thing on everyone's mind.

THE MAN HADN'T forgotten about him, though. He couldn't have. The two of them had grown very close since they met and would see each other regularly when he was around. In fact, they ended up becoming intimate with each other. He, the man, didn't really know what to call it, whatever was going on between them. Or rather it was he, the other one, who didn't, and the man just went along with that, out of deference to him. Because to the man it was all very clear: he was in love with him. To the other one, however, it wasn't, or at least so he claimed—he didn't like to talk about it, so it would have been hard for the man to know, and on the rare occasions when he did, he never spoke of love, or at least he never used that word. He used other words, some of which came close to it, just not that one.

§

In any case, the man hadn't forgotten about him. He thought about him all the time and was anxiously awaiting his return.

§

It made sense to assume, given the fact that there was something going on between them—even if they weren't entirely in agreement about what that might be—that the man would know what the other one was up to while he was gone. He didn't, though. They spoke about many things, just not about that. Clearly, that was also something he didn't like to talk about. Once, the man tried to get him to do that, but he refused. He said he didn't know how to yet. One day he might. For now, however, he didn't.

§

The man found himself returning to those words in the months after the war broke out. It seemed to him that if he'd known what the other one was up to, he would have been able to figure out where he was—and not only that but, depending on where he was, whether he was still around. People were dying in large numbers, the man said, and with each passing day, he couldn't help but wonder whether he had met the same fate.

FINALLY, ALMOST SIX months after they'd last seen each other, he got in touch. He told the man he was in the capital—he'd just gotten back and would like to see him. They met, and for the first time, when the man asked him where he'd

been and what he'd been doing, he gave
him an answer.

§

He said he'd been on the front lines. Not
fighting, though. Instead, he'd been wandering among the villages scattered across
the area. He said he'd been going there
since before the war. That was where he'd
been during those periods when he would
suddenly go missing. He'd known early on
that something was coming—he'd been
paying attention. Unlike most people, he
hadn't ignored the signs. When he learned
what was happening in those villages, he
decided to make his way over there. He
told the man that he'd gone there as a wit-
ness. At first, that had seemed enough.
Soon, however, he realized it wasn't. He
needed to do something, to help in some
way. The problem was that he didn't know
what someone like him had to offer. He
wasn't going to join in the fight. He'd end

up dead fairly quickly, and that clearly wouldn't be of much help. Then he remembered the years he'd spent training as an actor. He thought about everything he'd learned during that time, and it occurred to him that he could perhaps stage a play. He didn't know it at the time, but that was what he would end up doing. In the time he'd been wandering around those villages, he'd probably staged dozens of plays—he'd lost count of the exact number, but he was certain it was somewhere around that. The idea, he said, was to help people come to terms with what was happening. That was the criterion by which he chose what to stage. Everyone was welcome to participate, and not just as actors. There were all sorts of technical roles for people to fill, even though the productions (if one could call them that) were very simple—there was a war going on, so one really couldn't expect much from them.

§

One thing he took pains to emphasize was that the plays weren't really directed by him, not in the strict sense of the word. He'd oversee things at the beginning, but as soon as everyone knew what they were doing, he'd step back and let it all unfold on its own terms. It was all meant to be a communal endeavor. No single individual, least of all him, could take credit for it.

§

Of course, most of those villages were very small to begin with, and often when he arrived, he'd find only a handful of people in them—a large number of those who hadn't fled would have already been killed. So it was not uncommon for the plays to have no audience. Often it was just the whole village, or rather what was left of it, performing a play, essentially for no one.

HE DID THAT for almost two years. He'd be gone for a few months. Then, one day, he'd return to the capital. He'd get in touch with him—he'd call him on the phone and ask him if he wanted to meet. The man would never say no. A few days later, he would be gone again.

§

One time he had to take care of something. As a result, he ended up staying longer than he usually did. The war was raging at that point, and there were rumors that the capital would soon be bombed. The man proposed going on a trip to the coast, to the town we were in. The other one had never been there. He claimed he'd never really liked the sea. The man insisted. They could stay at the complex. No one was going anywhere at that point, and not just on account of the war—it was also the middle of winter. The man was sure they would be able to find a room in one of the hotels.

§

He didn't want to go. He didn't believe in the rumors. He thought the capital was safe. He intended to return to the front lines as soon as he could. In the end, though, he agreed. The man told him about the complex. He described it to him in great detail, and that was enough to spark his curiosity.

§

It was a strange trip. The complex was deserted. The two of them were the only guests. The town was also empty. A number of the buildings had even been boarded up. Only a handful of places were open, so they had to eat most of their meals in the hotel. On top of that, it was very cold. Neither one of them felt like going outside. They spent most of their time at the indoor pool and in the main lounge, drinking and listening to the music coming from the player piano in the lobby.

§

They soon began to feel claustrophobic. The staff's behavior only made things worse. They had nothing to do, so they followed them around wherever they went, constantly asking them if they needed anything. One morning, the two of them decided to go on a walk. Without intending to, they ended up at the salt pans. Out of the blue, he started speaking about some of the things he'd seen on the front lines, horrible things he'd rather forget. The man tried to warn him about the danger he was in, wandering around the area like that. He'd been lucky so far, but that could change at any moment. He wouldn't listen to him, though. He felt, he said, as if he had no choice but to go there.

§

They returned to the capital. A few days later, he was gone. Months went by. The war entered its most critical phase. The rumors turned out to be true. The capital was bombed. During that time, the man was constantly reading about a massacre in some village. Each time he did, he wondered if he might be among the dead, killed and then dumped into a mass grave in the middle of the forest. He didn't want to admit it, but he was almost certain that he was.

THE WAR CAME to an end one day, to everyone's surprise. It had seemed, at times, that it would drag on forever.

§

In the months that followed, even though he believed him to be dead, the man held on to the hope that he might soon hear from him. He would rather not have done that, but he kept reading about people who were thought to have died and who suddenly showed up at their front steps. It was mainly people who'd been fighting and had ended up being taken prisoner. Now that the war was over, they were all being released.

§

Late one night, his phone rang. The man had been out all day and had just gotten home. For a while, he just stood there, staring at the phone and letting it ring. By then it had been almost a year since he'd last seen him. Finally, the man picked up. No, he joked, it wasn't his ghost calling. He hadn't died and come back to haunt him. He was still very much alive. He was in the capital and was wondering if the man would like to meet.

§

They got together the following morning, and although on the phone he'd said he wasn't a ghost, he could have easily been mistaken for one. He looked very pale. He'd also never been so thin. He was basically nothing but skin and bones.

§

Among other things, the man learned that the building he used to live in had been severely damaged during the bombings. It was being demolished, so he had nowhere to go. Naturally, the man told him he could stay with him.

HE STRUGGLED TO adjust to the new reality. Everyone did, the man said, to one extent or another, but he seemed to have a harder time than most people. Things were very different from what they had been. For one, and as I already knew, the country they'd grown up in didn't exist anymore—

both of them were now citizens of a new country, one that in their minds had always been their country, even if it didn't officially exist. But now it did. Needless to say, that felt very strange. On top of that, and as the man had mentioned earlier, while he was telling me about the woman and her drawings, the years immediately following the end of the war were a period of great prosperity for the country. That was probably what he had the hardest time adjusting to. Life just seemed incredibly frivolous to him, which made perfect sense, considering everything he'd witnessed on the front lines. As he often told the man, he felt alienated from everyone around him. He couldn't partake in their giddiness—it didn't seem right to do so. He felt, he said, like an unwanted guest.

§

The irony is that, right around that time, people started to take an interest in him.

Certain people, at least. Stories of all kinds had been circulating for a while, about him and the things he had been doing, both before and during the war. Eventually, they reached the ears of a group of young art historians, who were immediately intrigued. As I might recall, he'd once told the man that he had a vision for the kind of work he wanted to do as an artist. He'd then gone on to say—I probably remembered that too—that he didn't feel ready to execute it yet and that he still had a lot to learn. These young art historians were fascinated by the way he'd gone about doing that. They'd never heard of a sentimental education like his—those were the exact terms they used, in a small pamphlet they would devote to him. Unsurprisingly, perhaps, given the fact that they were young, they also found themselves at odds with the critical establishment, specifically with the terms in which art was being discussed. This, the man said, was right around the time when the woman started to gain recognition for her drawings—critics, as he'd explained to me, were arguing at that point that art could, and should, have a strong political message. These young art historians, however, didn't want anything to do with that debate. They were searching for a completely new set of categories, and they thought that what he'd been doing might lay the groundwork for that, so long as the stories that had reached their ears were true.

§

The stories were true. It took some time, the man said, but they were eventually confirmed. As it happened, they differed in important ways from what he'd told him. For example, it turned out that he'd been on the front lines, but only after the war broke out. Before that, during those times when he would suddenly go missing, he'd been somewhere else. He'd been traveling, often to faraway places. It turned out too that while he was in those places, he had gotten himself into all kinds of situations— situations with other men, to be precise. These were men he met along the way, and getting himself into those situations with them was exactly what he was after. He'd gone to those places with that specific purpose in mind. That had been his aim.

§

Apparently, he'd been doing something similar during the war. In other words, and contrary to what he'd told the man, he hadn't been staging plays in the villages on the front lines. He'd been in that area, wandering around those villages, that much was true, but he hadn't been doing what he said he'd been doing. Some other artist had done that, a while back and in a different context. That artist was someone he admired, and he'd decided to say he'd been doing something similar after reading about it in a biography of him. But he hadn't. He'd actually been doing the same thing he'd been doing before the war. Only the setting had changed. Before the war he'd traveled to various places, while during the war he'd decided to restrict his activities to the front lines, to the villages scattered across the area and to the surrounding forests. The overall context (by which the man meant the war) had also been different—very different, to say the least. His activities, however, had been basically the same.

§

He'd lied to him, the man said. However, that didn't really bother him. He'd never been one to judge, and he trusted that he had his reasons for doing so. He suspected that he wanted to speak about what he'd been up to and that he would also rather not. Lying, the man said, had been his way of doing both.

§

Not that he had wanted it all to remain a secret. According to the man, something else that the art historians learned was that he'd recorded everything in a notebook. Every single one of the situations he'd gotten himself into, both before and during the war, had been meticulously documented. Granted, the existence of that notebook wasn't by itself proof that he wanted it all to come to light, as he could have chosen to destroy it. He didn't, though. He just hid it, in the bathroom of a rest stop, of all places, a spot he'd frequented at one point. He tucked it behind a urinal, where someone later found it. However, as he explained to the man one day, although when he put it there he was fully aware that someone might find it, he'd also thought that it was equally likely that no one would, and that even if someone did, it would probably be thrown away. The decision to record everything, then, hadn't been made with anyone else in mind. The notebook was never meant to be read, not by anyone other than himself, at any rate. He just wanted to have a place where he could put some things down in writing. As he told the man, he thought that this might help him reach a better understanding of what he was doing, and of everything he was learning as well.

§

Perhaps he believed that it was ultimately beyond his control, whether what he'd been doing would one day come to light, and that destroying the notebook wouldn't really make much of a difference. If that was the case, the stories that started to circulate proved him right. For that was how those art historians ended up learning about him. He might not have wanted to speak about any of it; others, though, clearly did, possibly some of the men he'd gotten himself into those situations with. This was not surprising since those situations had all been rather strange, and hence something that those men, like anyone involved in a situation of that sort, would probably have wanted to discuss. Still, he didn't want any of it to come out, regardless of whether that was within his control or not. The very nature of his activities, he explained to the man one day, was such that they risked being misunderstood.

THE MAN WANTED to make sure I didn't think, having heard him say that the other one had gotten himself into certain kinds of situations, that there had been something fortuitous about that. To the contrary, he'd gone in search of those situations—that was the reason why he went where he went, both before and during the war. The man had already made that clear, but it was worth repeating since most people wouldn't do something like that. Most people, the man said, might find themselves in those kinds of situations, but they wouldn't get themselves into them on purpose.

§

He, however, did. Very deliberately, he got himself into situations that most people would only want to find themselves in, if they really had no other choice but to experience them. Because most people wouldn't want to experience them. And not wanting to experience them, they wouldn't seek them out the way he did.

§

As the man had already noted, they were all rather strange situations. That had been true from the start, in other words, since before the war. But of course during the war they became even stranger, just as he had hoped would happen. Indeed, if once the war broke out he went to the front lines, it was in order to get himself into stranger, one could even say bizarre, versions of the situations he'd been getting himself into. This was all very clearly spelled out in that notebook, the one he ended up hiding in the bathroom of a rest stop.

§

That notebook was the main source for everything that came to be known about his activities—and possibly the only real source, the man said, since the stories that began circulating at one point were just rumors, and rumors weren't, strictly speaking, sources; the art historians who took an interest in him, for example, wouldn't have regarded them as such, even if it was those stories that first put them on his trail. The notebook, by contrast, was a document in the true sense of the word. He himself liked to refer to it as a chronicle—a chronicle of his own degradation, to be precise. That was ultimately what he was interested in, the one thing all the situations he'd gotten himself into had in common. They were all very degrading, in some cases extremely degrading, situations.

§

He was interested, however, not in degradation as such, but in how it made him feel, or rather in how it could make him feel—if the situations he got himself into had anything to teach him, it was about his capacities in that regard. For just when he thought he'd exhausted the range of possible feelings, he'd find himself feeling something he'd never felt before. Having gotten himself into one of those situations, it was not uncommon for an entirely new feeling, rather than a more intense version of an old, familiar feeling, to suddenly take possession of him.

§

Those feelings were far from pleasant. That went without saying, given the nature of the situations that gave rise to them. Over time, though, he discovered that they were too elusive to be categorized in any way, least of all as pleasant or unpleasant. They might be too elusive even to be known. No one, in fact, knew what a feeling was. He, of all people, was in a position to say that. After all, as a philosophy student, the question of what a feeling was had been one of his main preoccupations. He'd read everything he'd been able to find on the subject, assuming that someone out there must have come up with a satisfactory answer— that seemed to be true in the case of every other question. But no one had. None of the philosophers he'd read, at any rate, had. If he ended up getting himself into those situations, it was in part because of that. He just had to find out.

HE DEVISED A protocol. Having gotten himself into one of those situations, he would pay close attention to what he felt. Each feeling would be examined in detail. Once it had been identified, its qualities and fluctuations would be meticulously recorded and dissected.

§

That was the plan, at least. It wouldn't be long before he found himself wondering why he thought he might succeed where others had failed. Feelings, he came to realize, might indeed resist knowledge altogether. So he wrote in his notebook, during one of his more philosophical moments. It was the analysis to which he had subjected them (or rather tried to subject them) that led him to that insight. He would set out to scrutinize a feeling, but he would never manage to seize hold of it the way he thought he should, if his examination was to yield anything of substance. It was almost as if the very attempt to seize hold of the feeling, just so he could examine it, caused it to dissolve, leaving him with nothing. Clearly, if that was the case, it couldn't be his fault. He wasn't doing anything wrong, not as far as he could tell. He was dealing with something very unstable, a disturbance, evanescent and fleeting, arising out of conditions that, by their very nature, were themselves also ephemeral. Something of that sort was bound to evade all grasp.

§

The notebook was actually full of such philosophical moments. He indulged in them often enough to have persuaded the man that what he once said to him was true, and that when all was said and done, he might never have been anything other than a philosophy student. He had remained one, in fact, even after he abandoned his studies. He had abandoned his studies when he still had a long way to go—he was humble enough to recognize that. Nonetheless, by that point, he had already learned an important lesson, arguably the most important lesson that a philosophy student can learn. He had learned that what he sought to know might in the end lie beyond knowledge, and that in that case one should refrain from saying anything about it—beginning, of course, with what it is. Feelings were no exception, and it might be that the philosophers he'd read as a student were aware of this, not those who'd attempted to define and explain them, obviously, but those who hadn't said anything: their silence, he realized, might have had a different meaning than the one he'd assigned to it.

§

What feelings were, he discovered, was perhaps less important than what they demanded of one. It was crucial, he wrote, in another one of those philosophical moments, to relate to them in a manner that was consistent with their nature—he was thinking, specifically, of their elusiveness. It was primarily a matter of restraint—one should, at all times, refrain from making any assertions about them. No predicates of any sort were to be assigned to them under any circumstances—that was essentially what it all came down to. Words could wield a potent magic, rarely for the good. In a way, he'd known that all along. He'd sensed, early on, that it wasn't right to say, of the feelings that arose in him, that they were pleasant or unpleasant. But now he understood why that was so. Not saying something like that (not saying anything, for that matter) made it possible for them to dissipate, which was ultimately what feelings wanted to do. Asserting something about them had the opposite effect. He was speaking from his own experience, having by then perfected his capacity, amidst whatever might be happening, to shift his attention inward. He liked to think of himself as a sentinel, stationed at the edge of the vast expanse where feelings swirl in and out of existence. He'd been charged with observing them, and that was precisely what he'd been doing. He knew, therefore, that they would harden into something heavy and dense the moment he assigned them a specific attribute. Not long after that, gravity, whose effects they'd been spared, would exert its pull, drawing them down into the depths of the space that opened in front of him. He couldn't see into those depths, not all the way, at any rate, but he knew that they would settle there, sinking softly into sediments that, over time, would accumulate, eventually exerting enough pressure on themselves for them to fuse, permanently, into a compact crust. The notebook was full of descriptions of a vast and barren wasteland, a landscape in which, aside from the sky, that crust was all one could see. It was how he liked to picture death. No doubt he'd been thinking about the salt pans, the man said. As I already knew, he'd been there with him, and his description of the bone-white patches of land and of its cracked surface, slowly lighting up under the setting sun, resembled what they'd both seen at the time.

IT WASN'T UNTIL the war that he grasped this fully. Previously, he'd only been able to catch a glimpse of it. That made sense, considering that during the war he was tested in ways he hadn't been before, in terms of how much he could endure. The situations he got himself into

190

were such that it became almost impossible for him not to give in to the temptation to assert something about the feelings they elicited—to declare, even if only to himself, that they were not simply unpleasant, but utterly distressing. For some reason, it seemed to him that doing so might bring him some relief.

§

I knew that he hadn't been staging plays in the villages on the front lines—the man had already made that clear. Even if that had been his intention, he wouldn't have been able to do so, since most of the villages would have already been razed to the ground by the time he got to them. More than once, he happened to show up just a few hours later. That made him wonder if he had some sort of gift—as he wrote in the notebook, it was as if he knew where he needed to go in order to find them. That had been his aim from the start. He'd been searching for them since he first got there. He'd learned over time that there were certain signs he could trust: a smoldering building, a pack of dogs rummaging through the rubble, a car stopped in the middle of the road with its doors open and the engine still running. It was always thrilling, upon approaching a village, to catch sight of one of them. It meant that they were close by, possibly even there. Still, he would always force himself to wait until the sun had set. He wanted it to be dark by the time he went in and started wandering through the streets. That seemed fitting, for reasons he would only understand later.

§

In the darkness, he had only his ears to guide him. From time to time, he would hear their voices, rising above the crackle of the fires blazing all around him. In the notebook, he wondered why they always

192

seemed surprised to see him. They'd be huddled around a fire, drinking and talking, but as soon as they saw him they all fell silent. The majority of them came from faraway places, some of which he'd been to before the war, during those trips he made, so he'd usually be able to say a few words in whatever language they spoke. Just a few, though, definitely not as many as would have been necessary to let them know what he was doing there. But that could be conveyed in other ways. Words weren't really necessary for that. The fact that he wasn't wearing any clothes, for example—that already said a lot, if not everything.

§

He had often wondered about that strange habit of his of lurking in the shadows, waiting in the forest until the sun had set before entering a village. He didn't know why he did that, but it felt right to him, and that was really all that mattered. It became obvious to him after some time had passed that if he'd acted any differently, they might not have looked at him the way they did, as if he reminded them of something. That struck him as crucial, even if what he reminded them of wasn't all that clear—and it wasn't, not at first, at least. Surprisingly, it all turned out to be very simple, embarrassingly simple, actually: he reminded them of themselves. He was, he realized one day, a mirror of sorts—when they looked at him, it was really their own reflection they were seeing. This was not the result of some shared physical attribute. Most of them, as the man had already explained, came from faraway places, so he looked nothing like them. The resemblance lay elsewhere, in his relationship to the darkness. He was under the impression that they believed he'd issued from it, in a very literal sense. In other words, he hadn't been hiding in it. Instead, the darkness had spawned him. He was its product. His birth, however, could not be explained by reference to an external agent. He hadn't been fashioned by a demiurge, for which the darkness had served as raw material, nor had a force infused the darkness with something it didn't possess, fertilizing it, as it were. Instead, he'd come into being as a result of a transformation that the darkness itself had undergone, the way some liquids will coagulate under certain conditions. The reasons that precipitated that weren't clear. What was clear was that he was on intimate terms with the darkness, as one is bound to be with what has engendered one. His nakedness couldn't help but emphasize that. It really was no different, he wrote, from the nakedness of a newborn. At the same time, the special circumstances of his birth clearly set that intimacy apart, since he hadn't only been engendered by the darkness but was truly one with it. If they saw themselves reflected in him, it was on account of that. For they might not have been on intimate terms with the darkness proper, like he was, but they were on intimate terms with something for which the darkness was, at the very least, an apt symbol. He was talking about whatever it was that had descended upon that part of the world, causing so much destruction and suffering. He wasn't sure what to call it. He didn't believe there was such a thing as evil. The reality was always more complicated. Ignorance, perhaps, came closer to it. Either way, he knew not only that they were on intimate terms with it, but also that there was something oppressive about that intimacy—he knew how heavily it weighed on them. Perhaps they thought that he was there to help them. If they did, he wrote, they weren't wrong. That ignorance needed to be driven away, and he had vowed to do what he could to make sure it was. He would often picture it to himself, a viscous sludge they carried within them and were anxious to expel. He'd take it in—they could count on that. In fact, he'd do so eagerly, like a demon that has been deprived of sustenance for too long.

IT SHOULD COME as no surprise that he felt tested, day after day, or rather night after night, to an extent he'd never felt before. Indeed, for the very first time since he started getting himself into those kinds of situations—in other words, since before the war—he thought that it might be time for him to stop.

§

What he was doing was necessary, though. The men, at least, seemed grateful. After they were done with him, there was always a moment of silence. It was just a moment, but it felt endless. The silence, too, had a special quality. It was deep and comforting at the same time. He could tell that they appreciated what he'd done for them. They never would have said that, obviously. They never would have thanked him explicitly. And even if they had, he probably would not have been able to understand them. As the man had already explained, his knowledge of their language would have been rudimentary at best.

§

There were other reasons to think they were grateful. The way they looked at him during that silence, for example, the flicker of tenderness in their eyes. They always ended up regretting this momentary weakness, but the way they made that clear was in itself quite revealing. They would reach out for his face and start caressing it, sometimes even holding him by the chin for a brief moment before abruptly shoving him away, often with a look of disgust. That was how they'd return him to the darkness he seemed to have issued from, the darkness that had briefly lent him to them.

§

He would make his way back into the forest, and as he disappeared into it, he would feel grateful, too. For he'd been given a chance to be of some benefit to them, which he appreciated, even if he also felt conflicted—understandably, given that, in all honesty, he'd been following an impulse that was far from altruistic, an impulse to frequent places of the kind he'd been wandering around for quite a while now, frightening places where he could expect to get himself into equally frightening situations, all for the sake of what he might learn from them. He'd been following that impulse from the very beginning, in other words, since before the war. That, he wrote, was exactly what he'd been doing all along. The only difference was that, during the war, the places he frequented became not just frightening but at times truly terrifying. The same was true of the situations he got himself into. The notebook he'd kept was nothing (aside from all the other things he liked to say it was, a chronicle of his own degradation being one of them) but a record of his attempts to follow that impulse, even when it led him into situations he probably should have avoided. He never avoided them, but that wasn't enough for him to believe he had succeeded. To the contrary, he was convinced he had failed. That was what he often told the man. He would have liked to think that he'd gone as far as he could. But he hadn't, or so it seemed to him, judging, again, the man said, by what he wrote. For he had come back in the end, whereas if he'd gone as far as he could, he probably wouldn't have.

HE STRUGGLED TO adjust to the new reality—the man had already pointed that out. But it didn't fully capture what was going on inside him, since the truth was that he disapproved of that reality. He found it repulsive. He really had no intention of adjusting to it—that was a concession he wasn't willing to make. At the same time, he didn't like feeling that way. He recognized that it went against everything he'd learned. He was aware, also, that at any moment his aversion could spiral into arrogance.

§

He wasn't sure what to do with himself, and for a while, he toyed with the idea of returning to his thesis, the one he'd left unfinished. A project like that, he thought, might at the very least distract him from what he was feeling. However, he didn't get very far with it. As he told the man, it was too hard for him to focus on anything. Nothing could really hold his attention for very long.

§

One day, the man walked into his apartment and found a note. In it, he wrote that he'd realized that it was time for him to disappear. Not the way he had done in the past—in other words, for a period of time, which, no matter how long, would eventually come to an end. Instead, he'd be disappearing for good. He wasn't planning to start a new life somewhere else or anything like that. His intention, rather, was to die.

§

He went back to the front lines, the man was sure of that. No one had heard from him since, and his body had never been found, but there was no reason to think that he'd gone anywhere else. The man didn't know what kind of death he'd chosen. His guess was that he'd decided to starve himself. It made sense, especially if he hoped to be done with it quickly—he was already so frail.

§

Interestingly, when explaining his decision to disappear, he would end up echoing the language the woman had used—in the note, he, too, spoke of a retraction. As he put it, he was retracting his whole existence, or rather, his whole existence was being retracted—a passive construction felt more fitting to him, given the fact that death was involved. He liked to think of that retraction as making room for something else, whatever that might be, he himself didn't really know.

§

And yet, the man said, though he'd chosen to disappear, he'd also wanted it to seem as though he'd been buried somewhere. As he wrote, also in the note he left, anyone who in the future wished to visit his grave should be able to do so—with a touch of irony he went on to add that, if things continued to go the way they'd been going, his grave might one day become something of a pilgrimage site. He wasn't wrong to think that. Every now and then, people would pay him a visit. Not that many, though, at least not anymore. He'd been talked about, but only for a while. Even the art historians who took an interest in him would eventually move on— some even turned against him, the man said. Not that it mattered. In fact, they shouldn't have taken an interest in him in the first place. So he liked to say—he'd come to think of it as a big misunderstanding. By that point, he no longer considered himself an artist. He'd set out to learn what he thought he needed to learn in order to become one, but that ended up having an effect he never would have foreseen. As he said to the man one day, the preparations had killed the aspiration. Somewhere along the way, he'd abandoned the idea, without ever looking back. His grave, however, continued to attract visitors. The man knew that to be the case because often when he came he found all sorts of things on top of it, things people liked to leave as offerings: flowers, pebbles, bracelets. This time there hadn't been anything there, just those dead leaves he'd brushed off earlier, but that wasn't usually the case. No, he hadn't been forgotten. That sounded too much as if he'd been wronged in some way, when the reality was simply that he'd become a thing of the past and was now fading gradually into oblivion, much like everything else once it is lost to time. He never doubted that he was destined to fade away completely—much like everything else, too—and that made it difficult, the man said, to know how he truly felt about the prospect of people visiting his grave. As he wrote in the note, he understood why one would insist, when confronted with the stark reality of death, that something remained. Visiting someone's grave was no doubt a way of doing that. It was, he wrote, yet another example of our ten-dency to hold on to things no matter what. Even when we know them to be on their way to becoming nothing, we fail to recognize them as illusions, which is exactly what they are. Our bodies and the bodies of those around us were no exception. Even before life had deserted them—and all the more so afterward—they were nothing more than that. This, he once told the man, had become very clear to him during his time on the front lines—had that not been the case, he might not have been able to go through any of it. Knowing that, he felt as though he'd already given his body away, so that it didn't really matter what others did with it. Still, he understood the impulse. He understood why one would continue to cling to an illusion. He wasn't above that. He wasn't above anything, for that matter. He was just like everybody else. His own failure, he wrote, had made that obvious to him.

§

There was more to it, though. In the note, he declared that, in spite of everything, it might be fitting, in this particular case, for others to believe, and to insist, that something remained. What he wrote in connection with this was somewhat difficult to understand—the rest of the note was nowhere near as cryptic. As he put it, if something remained, then he couldn't be said to have faded away completely. He was still here, in a way. That might not have been what he believed, but it didn't contradict his willingness to come back and do it all over again, if that ever became necessary.

§

The grave before us didn't exactly belong to him. He'd come across it while walking around the cemetery in the months before he disappeared for good. He'd made a trip to the town one day—he'd wanted to visit the complex where he and the man had spent a few days while the war was raging, and to walk around the salt pans as well. Once he was done with that, he'd wandered into the cemetery. This was very unusual since he really disliked cemeteries— the man knew that to be the case because he'd said so to him one day. They were in the capital, on their way somewhere. The man told him they'd get there faster if they cut through the main cemetery, but he refused. He said that the idea of going into a cemetery made him uncomfortable, though not for the reasons one might think—he wasn't afraid of the dead or anything like that. It had something to do with his time on the front lines. Having been there, cemeteries just seemed ludicrous to him. He was thinking of all the bodies he'd seen, piled on top of one another at the bottom of some pit. Compared to that, cemeteries looked almost like resorts. That may have been the reason why he ended up in the cemetery that day. He'd been at the complex so he might have wanted to see if what he'd said to the man that day was true, if the complex and the cemetery were indeed similar in some way, the man wasn't completely sure but he suspected as much. Regardless, he'd gone in. The cemetery was very quiet. (It always was, despite the fact that it contained some important graves—most visitors, the man said, stuck to the promenade and the main square.) He'd been wandering around for some time, going down the various paths at random. The grave caught his attention right away. The plaque on the stone indicated that a man lay buried there—a man who, coincidentally, had died at the same age he was then. Back in the capital, he'd tracked down his descendants, two nieces living together in a home for the elderly. They barely remembered their uncle, who'd died when they were both still very young. He offered them some money, in exchange for which they allowed him to replace the original plaque with one bearing his name and the dates of his birth and of his death. (Obviously, he couldn't have known when he was going to die, but he did know when he was going to disappear—he'd planned things very carefully—so he decided to list that day as the date of his death.) He didn't want the body lying under the stone to be disturbed in any way. He just wanted the plaque changed. In that way, anyone who cared to visit his grave would be able to do so, though it would be no secret that it was really someone else who lay there. Still, the plaque would make it seem like he was there, even though he wasn't. And so there we were, the man said, where he really wasn't.

THE MAN AND I stood quietly in front of the grave. Then the man started walking. I followed him, past a small metal gate leading out of the cemetery and into a garden adjoining a church. The man made his way toward a balustrade on the far end. Once in front of it, he placed both hands on the top rail and leaned over. I did the same, as soon as I was by his side.

§

Below us, a stone wall plunged several hundred feet directly into the sea. Without lifting his gaze, the man explained that we were looking at a remnant of the defensive wall that had once encircled the town. I knew we had climbed to the top of a hill, but I still wouldn't have thought we were that high up.

§

The man and I stared at the waves below. We must have done that for a while—by the time we both looked up again, the sun was about to set. Lights were flickering in the distance, on the opposite side of the bay. The man asked me if I could make out the village I currently live in. He tried to point it out to me, but it was hard for me to see much of anything because of the haze. Turning to his right, he then gestured toward a flat expanse of land at the bottom of a cliff. The salt pans, he said, lay just past it.

§

I leaned over the balustrade again. The sea was a bright blue color, and the water near the shore was so clear I could see all the way down to the pebbles on the seafloor. My mood had shifted; I felt oddly calm. The unease that had gripped me earlier had faded. I knew it was still somewhere inside of me, but it seemed to have retreated to a faraway corner, like a creature in need of rest. I wanted to make sure it remained undisturbed, so I didn't say anything. Neither did the man, and I was grateful to him for that.

§

At some point, the man said we should get going. I assumed he would be dropping me off in the village near the border, and I said something to that effect, but he replied that under no circumstances would he be doing that. It was too late; most likely, the bus I needed to take had already stopped running. He said he'd give me a ride home; he actually didn't mind the drive.

Duino, November 2023 -
New York, September 2025

ACKNOWLEDGMENTS

My first word of gratitude goes to my friends in the village of Duino, Italy, where I began to work on this book: Joanne de Koning, Khalid El-Metaal, Christoph Genz, Hristo Guertchev, Nayrie Kalayjian, Joni Mäkivirta, Matt Marinec, Giulia Postal, Aparna Ramchandran, Rimma Rapaporte, and Enea Zaramella. I am especially grateful to Miriam Nash, Laura Summers, Pablo Martínez Rosado, Toni Flego, Deni Pregelj, Francesco Zanchini, Fabio Lombardo, and Bostjan Vuga for the generosity and warmth with which they welcomed me into their lives.

I remain, as always, deeply grateful to the people who have supported me in my efforts to become a writer. I especially want to thank Mario Bellatin and Avital Ronell, and my friends Carolyn Ferrucci and Estelle Srivijittakar.

Finally, I would like to thank Jordan Kirk. This book is dedicated to him.

ABOUT THE AUTHOR

Christopher van Ginhoven Rey is a writer and a visual artist. *Retraction* is his first novel.